Oh, Good!

by Judy Nayer

illustrated by
Kathleen O'Malley

Scott Foresman

Editorial Offices: Glenview, Illinois • New York, New York
Sales Offices: Reading, Massachusetts • Duluth, Georgia
Glenview, Illinois • Carrollton, Texas • Menlo Park, California

I do not want this .

quilt

Oh, good!

I do not want this .

book

Oh, good!

I do not want this .

shirt

Oh, good!

I do not want this .

bunny

Oh, good!

I do not want this .
cup

Oh, good!

I do not want this .

hat

Oh, good!

All for me!

All for you?

No. All for you and me!